WHAT HAPPENS TO YOUR FOOD?

Alastair Smith

Illustrated by Maria Wheatley

Designed by Maria Wheatley and Ruth Russell

Digital artwork by John Russell

Series editor: Judy Tatchell

What is food for?

Without food, your body would stop working, like a car that has run out of fuel.

Food gives you energy to move around.

Food makes you grow bigger.

Food helps you stay strong and healthy.

Feeling hungry

When you are hungry, your stomach feels empty. It might make rumbling noises.

If you don't eat, the feeling of hunger grows and grows.

He needs food!

You might start to feel floppy and unhappy.

Your food's journey

After you swallow your food, it goes down a long, wiggly tube inside you.

The food slides down the wiggly food tube. It is broken up into tiny pieces.

Your body uses the tiny pieces to keep you going.

Just take a look inside!

The food tube starts at your mouth.

The food tube ends at the hole in your bottom.

3

What should you eat?

You need to eat different kinds of food. This keeps your body healthy.

Some foods are good for helping you to grow. They also help to mend cuts and bruises. Here are some of them.

Milk

Cheese

Fish

Eggs

Potatoes

Bread

Rice

Beans

Pasta

Some kinds of food are very good for giving you energy. You can see some of these above.

Your body needs vitamins and minerals. These keep it working well. Fruit and vegetables have lots of these.

Lettuce

Apples

Oranges

Tomatoes

Carrots

Strawberries

What shouldn't you eat?

You shouldn't eat things that have gone bad. Food goes bad when it gets old.

Also, beware of germs in food.

What are germs?

Germs are tiny creatures. They are too small for you to see. Some germs can make you ill if you eat them.

How can you get rid of germs?

Be a germ killer...

We love to live in meat and fish.

Please don't lift the flap!

Is it yummy?

How do you decide what you want to eat?

Look at it...

You decide whether you like the look of it.

Yuck!

Yum!

Remember it...

You remember what you thought of it last time you tasted it.

Smell it...

You decide whether you like the way it smells.

Taste it...

You decide whether you like the way it tastes.

Making food yummy

You can mix things together and cook them to make great new tastes.

Even making food look nice can help you to enjoy it.

Sauces or dressings can make things taste more interesting.

Taste test

How do you taste different things?

What happens in your mouth?

Your mouth is a food masher. It changes the things you eat into a slippery paste. This paste is easy to swallow.

Your teeth chop your food up into little pieces.

Your tongue pushes the food around inside your mouth.

Spit makes food soft and slippery. It slides down your throat.

About your teeth

You have different types of teeth. They do different jobs.

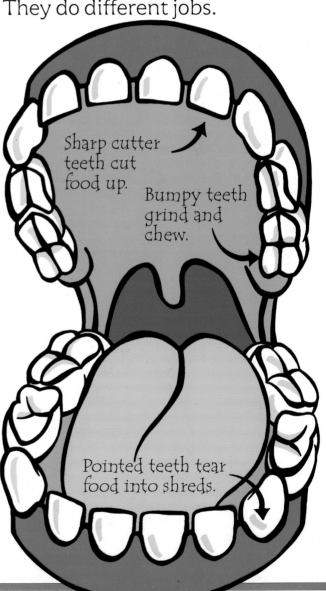

Sharp cutter teeth cut food up.

Bumpy teeth grind and chew.

Pointed teeth tear food into shreds.

How many teeth?

Newborn babies have no teeth. You grow your first teeth when you are a few months old. You grow 20 baby teeth.

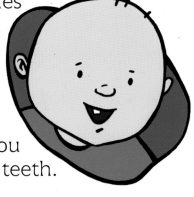

Your baby teeth start to fall out when you are about six. You grow 32 bigger teeth instead. These should last all your life.

Taking a bite

First you open wide, then ...

9

Into your stomach

Your food's next stop on its way down the food tube is in your stomach. This is like a squashy bag.

Where is your stomach?

Your stomach is about level with your elbows.

What does your stomach do?

Your stomach squeezes and mashes food up. It pours special stomach juices on the food. These help mush it up. It ends up like a slushy soup.

Food squirts out of your stomach here.

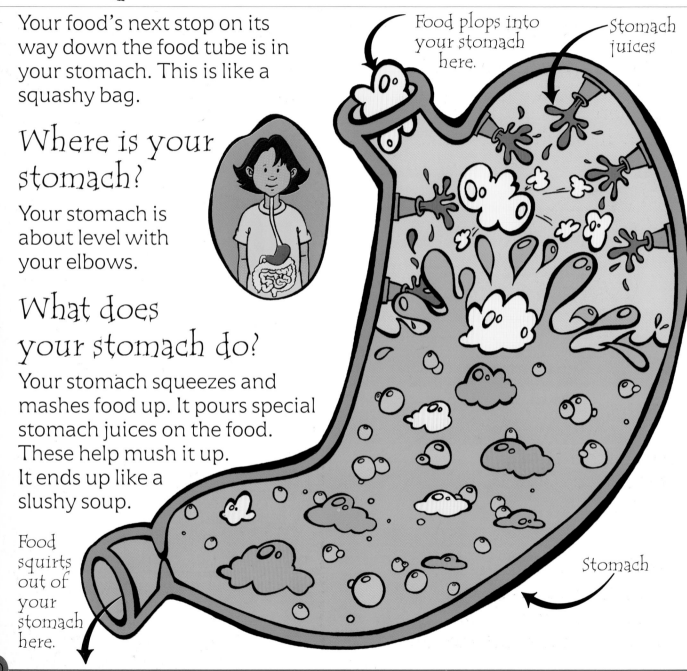

Food plops into your stomach here.

Stomach juices

Stomach

How big is your stomach?

If your stomach is empty it is about as big as this picture of a balloon. But your stomach can stretch to hold a big meal.

A grown-up's empty stomach is about twice as big as this picture of a balloon.

Eating too much

Sometimes you eat and drink too much. Your stomach might decide that it's had enough.

What happens next?

Where food goes next

The slushy food gets out of your stomach through a small hole. It squirts through the hole little by little.

Now it goes into a long, curled-up part of the food tube. This is your small intestine.

Moving along

The food tube squeezes food along all the way from your mouth to your anus.

It works like toothpaste being squeezed up a tube.

What's that noise?

After a meal you may hear gurgling noises coming from inside you. What's going on?

Gurgle

Bash

Mash

Don't worry, it's only your food being mashed and squeezed in your food tube.

In the small intestine

Here, special juices, called digestive juices, squirt onto the food. These dissolve the food pieces into even tinier pieces.

Digestive juices

Digestive juices turn the food into smaller pieces.

Stomach

The hole opens and closes to let food through. Here it is closed.

Where do the food pieces go next?

Let's get out of here!

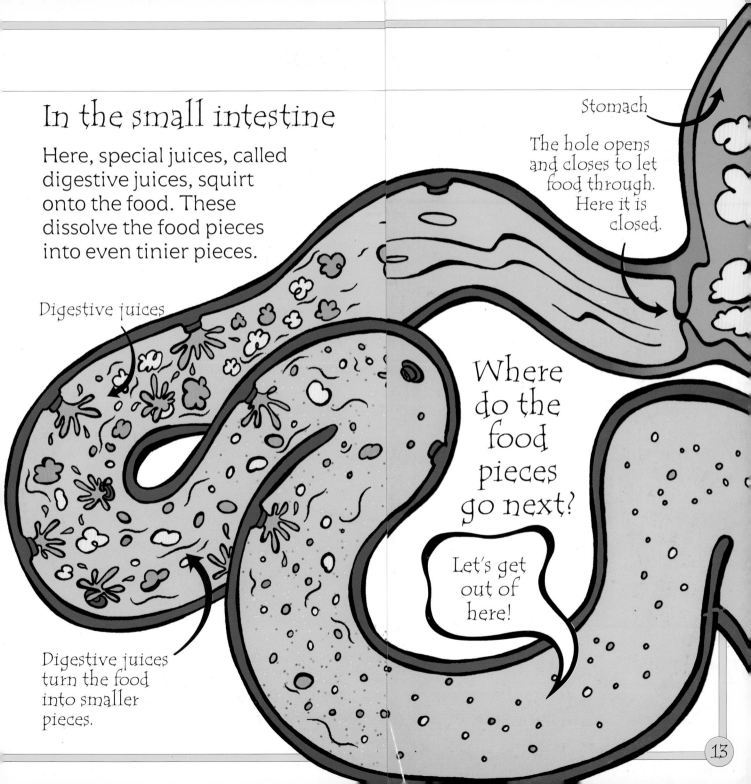

Journey's end

At the end of your small intestine, food is squeezed into the next part of the food tube. This is called the large intestine.

The large intestine is wider and shorter than the small intestine.

The large intestine ends at your anus.

What happens here?

The large intestine works like a sieve. It sucks water out of the sloppy food through its sides.

The food left behind gets more solid and sludgy as water drains out.

Sloppy food

Water comes out through the sides.